Don't Look Now

Brian Leon Lee

Brian Leon Lee

ISBN: 9798858664505
Imprint: Independently published

The Author

The author was born in Manchester. On leaving school, a period in accountancy was followed by a teaching career in Primary Education

Now retired and living in South Yorkshire.
Several years of telling his own stories to his then young children, led to the development of his many story characters, especially, Bouncey the Elf.

By Brian Leo Lee
(Children's Stories)

Bouncey the Elf and Friends Bedtime Stories
Just Bounce
Bouncey the Elf and Friends Meet Again
Bouncey the Elf and Friends (Box Set)

Mr Tripsy's Trip
Mr Tripsy's Boat Trip
Four Tales from Sty-Pen

**

By Brian Leon Lee

Trimefirst
Domain of the Netherworld
Spectre of El Dorado
The Club
Marco
Easy Meals Simply with Brian

(Paperback and eBooks}

Check for Free
Brian Leo Lee
eBooks
@
smashwords.com

For

Rita

Contents

Chapter 1.	1
Chapter. 2	4
Chapter 3	8
Chapter. 4	12
Chapter 5	15
Chapter. 6	20
Chapter 7	24
Chapter 8	27

1

The patch of giant ferns was a gift from heaven, even though they were sopping wet and as another stream of droplets fell onto the back of Chaz's neck, as he lay well-hidden underneath the big fronds, he shivered. Not from the cold dank, pungent odour of the undergrowth but from the sight of three apparitions from hell – man-vamps – flying in and out of the tall trees that surrounded the ferns in which he was hiding.

They were completely hairless and their human-like faces were casting about, looking. Looking for him.

The eyes were yellow orbs, a snub nose could barely be seen because of a large top-lip curled right back to expose a set of long canines.

Red tongues protruding like the heads of a small snake, were flicking in and out of their mouths in a sticky mess of drool and saliva.

Chaz could see that the wings, giant leathery wings, were attached to the back of their naked bodies that had a yellowish tinge. The hands and feet were of human shape and
proportions except for the claw like nails, which had transformed into long razor -sharp talons.

The beasts from hell flew nearer and Chaz drew back, praying that he hadn't been seen as they chittered to each other.

He flinched when the downdraft of the nearest one's huge flapping wings, wafted several fronds to and fro but it had suddenly veered away with a loud screech and the other two echoing it with cries of their own, followed.

They did not go far.

Peering furtively from under the safety of the large fern fronds, Chaz saw the reason for his possible reprieve.

A peasant with a full beard had entered the glade, dressed in a simple hemp white shirt, covered with an embroidered waistcoat, white cotton trousers with tied leggings, held up with a wide belt and wearing leather sandals and a sheepskin hat.

He was carrying three or four rabbits in one hand and a long, iron-shod staff in the other.

Before he had moved another ten paces, he was attacked by the three man-vamps. He froze in terror as he saw the grotesque apparitions falling through the air towards him. Gaping maws, full of fangs and emitting ear shattering shrieks fell upon him.

He had time for one wailing cry before he was knocked to the ground, raked by the wicked -

taloned hands and feet of the three monsters.

As the screaming peasant fell to the ground, the three man-vamps began to fight each other, wings flapping against each other until one slipped in the gore of the peasant and was forced away from him.

With triumphant shrieks the other two man-vamps pounced on the peasant and began to eat him.

That was what Chaz thought. Then he realised, they were not eating, they were drinking the peasant's blood.

My God, he thought in horror. 'The poor devil's having his lifeblood sucked from him by the giant vampires.'

Seizing his chance, Chaz slowly backed away and then crawled through the lower branches of the giant ferns until he reached the edge of the glade.

More shrieks and chittering from the man-vamps made him turn round. The third hideous creature had tried to force his way to the peasant's body and was being snarled at to keep away.

Knowing that the flapping grisly monsters wouldn't hear him. Chaz got to his feet and ran for his life.

2

Chaz stopped running and leaned forward, hands on his knees, gasping for breath.

'God,' he thought, *'I need to rest.'*

His heart rate began to slow down and gulping and coughing enough to think that it would never end, he stumbled over to a small stream that happened to be right next to where he had stopped.

Bliss.

He cupped his hands together again and dipped them into the rushing stream and drank more of the nectar of the Gods.

Felling much better, he knelt and splashed his face with cold water, then sat down on the edge of the stream and untied his trainers and took off his socks.

My God. Did it feel good to have his sweaty feet pushing small smooth pebbles around the streambed and watch swirls of mud and sand being carried away.

Chaz leaned back on his hands, content for the moment just to relax and get over the shock of seeing what those hideous man-vamps had done to that peasant.

'Jeez, that could have been me.'

He sat up quickly and looked around.

He had heard a strange noise coming from an

open space among the trees just across the stream from where he was sitting.

Sod drying my feet, he thought, as he pulled on his socks and tied his trainers.

He stood and then gasped aloud.

'What the hell is that?'

A wooden hut, the sort woodcutters used in this country, was walking around the open space he had noticed before.

Chaz was gobsmacked when he saw that there were four huge bird-type legs on each corner of the hut.

The incredible, mind-boggling hut stopped moving and bending the giant bird-legs, crouched down on the edge of the glade, a normal looking hut again.

Chaz began to roll his eyes in disbelief when the door of the hut opened and a hideous figure stepped outside holding a broomstick.

She, for it was woman, leaned against the doorway to catch her breath. The wide gaping mouth exposed two or three rotting teeth. A long, bulbous nose dribbled onto her upturned chin, which was covered in warts, several of which sprouted grey hairs.

The rest of her blotchy-mottled face was partly hidden by a set of straggly eyebrows, which screened a pair of mismatched squinting eyes.

Lank, lifeless hair hung down to her waist, giving a sense of false modesty to the dangling, drooping breasts that her filthy looking smock and shawl couldn't.

'Jeez, she must be a frigging witch,' Chaz muttered to himself.

The old woman squinted at Chaz, who hurriedly stepped behind the nearest tree.

'You can't hide from me' she cackled. 'What do you want from Mother Baba?'

Then with a grimace, which Chaz took for a smile, she said in a wily tone, 'Have you brought Mother Baba a present?'

Chaz peered again round the tree but before he could speak….

The broomstick suddenly jumped out of the old woman's hand and flew across the glade and whacked Chaz across his head before returning to her.

'Ouch!'

Mother Baba's mouth opened wide, showing her rotten teeth, just tiny gaping stumps and sniggered, 'Don't be keep me waiting young man or I might get angry.'

Thinking he had better say something, Chaz called back. 'I … I… I'm lost. I must have taken the wrong path.' 'Well don't stand there all day. Mother Baba is waiting. Come over and have a drink of my latest brew. I have just ladled a bowl to cool. Hurry now.' Mother Baba lifted the broomstick ominously. 'I'm getting cold….'

Just then a black cat came racing past the old women screeching and yowling before disappearing out of sight in the undergrowth.

But not before Chaz has seen that the head and chest of the cat was completely bald of fur.

'Come back you interfering moggy. I told you not to go near that bowl of cooling slug and unicorn-offal tea. I'll turn you into a ………'

Chaz didn't hear the rest of the old woman's threats. He had turned and ran away along the side of the stream, which fortunately then dropped down into a narrow gully.

3

Scrambling down as fast as he could safely weave his way between outcrops of wet rocks, Chaz rcached the bottom of the gully and stopped.

Not again, he thought, as his heaving chest sought to drag more air into his lungs.

He waited a few more minutes and after a drink of water, set off again not know where the hell he was going.

A rough path followed the side of the stream, which at least gave him some comfort. Somebody must be using this track, maybe he might get some help in getting out of this God forsaken place.

After a kilometre or two, Chaz found himself at the upper end of of a wooded valley and saw that the stream flowed into a large lake with an island more or less in the centre of it.

By now he was feeling knackered, so he sat down. His feet ached and he was hungry.

He suddenly wondered why he had no backpack and how the hell had he got here.

He felt a pang of fear.

This is ridiculous. My name is Chaz…. What'

My God! I can't even remember my frigging name.'

He looked frantically around.

Tree covered hills, the lake….

'Chuffin' hell, where the hell am I.'

He stood up, '*Come on Chaz, man up,*' he said to himself as he looked to see if there was anything he could eat.

Away from the stream, a grassy knoll merged into the woods that grew up the higher slopes of the valley. There among clumps of bracken he saw what he wanted.

Blueberry bushes grew up the sides of the knoll.

'Thank the Gods, at least I won't starve.' he said, as he climbed up to the nearest bushes.

Chaz was lucky. They were ripe, big and juicy, though of course because they are tiny compared to say, plums and don't grow in bunches like grapes, it took ages to eat enough to satisfy his hunger.

By then, his hands were covered with the red sticky juice from the berries. That jogged a memory, cooked blueberries produceda a red/purple coloured juice. Cooked or raw they both tasted great in his opinion.

Feeling much happier now, having eased his rumbling stomach, Chaz had to walk down towards the lake to wash his sticky hands.

The stream had widened as it reached the lake

and had formed mudflats in places covered with marsh grass and reeds.

Not a healthy place to walk, thought Chaz, as he walked on.

A bit further on he found the ideal spot. A tiny sandy beach shaded by a copse of silver birch trees with a grassy slope by the water's edge.

A small bank of reeds and rushes poked up between the jumble of rocks that jutted out of the water, giving the place a secretive presence.

This will do nicely, thought Chaz as he walked over and knelt down to rinse his sticky hands. As he stood to shake them dry, he noticed a small boat jammed amongst the reeds.

It was, when he walked over to get a closer look, some sort of homemade canoe. More like those hollowed out of tree trunks he had seen in foreign wild life films on TV. This one though, was covered in withered weeds and mud.

Suddenly, a squelching, gurgling sound came from behind him and a pair of slimy hands grabbed him round the neck and pulled him into the lake.

He just had time to get a glance of his attacker and wished he hadn't.

A face half covered by slime, algae encrusted hair, two slits where the nose should be and a pair of sunken, red eyes glared at him. The skin of the semi-naked body and arms felt like the scales of a fish.

Then, pulling Chaz up close to its hideous face, the creature snarled, showing a set of bony teeth, as it blew a puff of noxious breath into his face and Chaz fell unconscious.

4

The canoe edged closer to the island, making for a small cove that was partially hidden by steep cliffs, including the mouth of a cave, which was only accessible by water.

Eons ago, an underground river breached the cliffs and flowed into the lake.

The creature paddled into the cave and tied up next to a convenient ledge just above the water level.

Chaz was just about aware of what was happening but couldn't do a thing about it. He was paralysed.

He sensed being pulled out of the canoe and into the water. He nearly lost his mind when he was dragged under and thought he would drown but to his surprise found that he was breathing normally. Magic or not, he was just glad to be still alive.

Sometime later, he was unable to guess how long, he was pulled out of the water by the creature and left alone on a rocky outcrop.

Slowly the effect of the paralysis wore off and Chaz saw that he was in a water-filled cavern.

He was amazed to see that the dim lights dotted

around the cavern were in fact clumps of glowing fungi growing out of the rocky walls.

'Aagh.'

Chaz rolled over to one side clutching a leg. 'Jeez, what a time to get cramp.'

He grabbed the nearest large rock and pulled himself up and hopped up and down for a bit before putting his foot down and pushed as hard as he could.

The pain eased and then it was gone.

And so was his fuzzy headache, the stuff that had knocked him out had obviously gone for good.

Limping a little, Chaz followed a narrow trail he could just make out in the gloom of the cavern. It twisted and turned between the bigger rocks until it reached a fissure in the wall. A wooden door blocked the way but Chaz found that it wasn't locked, so he went through into a long tunnel, lit at intervals by the fungi-lights.

Not knowing what to expect, he made his way slowly along the tunnel listening for any sound that might warn him of any trouble.

After a few minutes he reached a junction with another tunnel.

Unfortunately for him, it was guarded by what Chaz would call a 'cousin' of the gruesome creature who had brought him the cavern.

It was small, about a metre high, with a large bald-domed head and elfin like ears. A tiny mouth, from which jutted a single tooth that looked like a stick of dried nasal mucus hanging from the bulbous nose.

But it was the eye that startled Chaz.

The guard stared with such intensity that only one with a huge single eye, could do.

That was enough to make Chaz stop in his tracks but when the eye began to glow and change colour as the creature started to chant, he felt afraid of what might happen next.

The chant quickened and the eye began to flicker faster and faster in time with it. Then a bright ray of light blinded Chaz for a second and then he felt drowsy and a strong desire to sleep.

5

'Come – follow me,' a voice in his head ordered and Chaz, all befuddled by what had happened to him, suddenly found his legs moving by themselves and in a trance - like manner, followed the one-eyed creature, whose eye was now back to normal.

A loud thud of a heavy door closing, jolted Chaz back to his senses. He was in a cell-like room carved out of rock, with no other opening than the door. bunch of plant- lights in a wall crevice, made it light enough to see by.

A pile of rotting rushes had been thrown into a corner, obviously for a bed. A clay jar containing some stale water and another larger one, empty, completed the room's furnishings.

Chaz shivered. '*What the hell have I got myself into,*' he thought to himself, as he lay down in his soaking wet clothes.

***

The cell door creaked open and Chaz, bleary-eyed, looked up. A one-eyed apparition appeared in the doorway.

'Jeez.' I wasn't dreaming after all,' whispered Chaz to himself.

The creature began to chant and the single eye began to change colour and an orange ray of light enveloped him.

'Follow me,' said a voice inside his head

Chaz got to his feet and with a blank expression on his face, followed the creature through a series of tunnels with a stiff-legged gait that made him sway like a drunk. He was totally oblivious of his situation.

He entered a large chamber, unaware that several peasants were working in it, some, each with a large pickaxe were hacking into the rock face at the far end.

Others, were carrying the quarried rock to a large wicker basket, which had been lowered through a hole in the top of the chambers by a vine-rope.

All of the peasants had the stupefying look of those controlled by the one-eyed creatures. Chaz was led into the chamber and handed over to a 'supervisor' or guard.

'Take this pickaxe and join the others,' a mental voice ordered.

Stumbling over loose rocks littering the floor of the chamber, Chaz joined the group hacking the rock face of the chamber.

He lifted the heavy pickaxe he had been given and swinging it high over his head, brought it down with a mighty swoosh.

Chaz had never used a pickaxe before and not being in control of his body, because of the creatures' powers, his pickaxe skidding off the rockface chipped a lump of rock out of it, sending it flying across the chamber straight into the eye of the guard.

With a loud scream, the guard fell to the floor of the chamber, his body twitching and writhing, then it was still. Chaz and the peasants suddenly became aware of being inside the chamber and the lifeless body of the guard.

The peasants dropped their pickaxes with loud shouts and cries –

WHERE ARE WE?

WHAT'S THAT? pointing to the creatures' dead body,

HOW CAN WE GET OUT OF HERE.?

Chaz was the first to see more creatures approaching the chamber and with fear in his eyes, anxiously looked round for a means of escape.

A creaking, groaning sound made him look round. The large wicker basket, half full of rocks, was being slowly hoisted by the vine-rope towards the hole in the roof.

Without a moments' thought, Chaz rushed across the chamber and leapt on top of the half - filled wicker basket, now a metre or so off the floor.

The swinging, twirling wicker basket was near the roof of the chamber when Chaz heard the sound of chanting.

'Jeez, not again.' Closing hie eyes, Chaz clung to the sides of the basket, ignoring the pain of a sharp rock jammed against his left thigh.

The sound of chanting became fainter as the half- filled wicker basket was pulled through the hole in the roof of the chamber.

Then Chaz felt the wicker basket swing across the hole and with a sudden jerk, it was still.

Holding tight, crouching low, Chaz looked around. The wicker basket was tilted on top of a mound of rocks and he could see several peasants jerkily approaching to empty the basket he was hiding in.

They were obviously under the influence of the creatures.

Chaz gave a gasp of horror. *There must be one of the here,* he thought.

As silently as he could, Chaz climbed out of the wicker basket, on the side away from the now, nearly on top of him, peasants, Fortunately for him, they were totally unaware of him as they woodenly, began to unload the rocks.

Looking around, Chaz picked a suitable rock, not too heavy but with sharp jagged edges from the pile he was standing on. He saw that the rocky pile was near the top of a small hill. Not so far away was a wood, *A good place to hide*, he thought.

What he feared happened, A creature guard suddenly appeared from the group of working peasants. It raised an arm and began to chant.

Chaz nearly froze with fear but somehow as he felt himself becoming drowsy, he threw his jagged rock. His aim was true, it hit the shining, single eye of the chanting creature.

It fell to the ground with a gurgling splutter and began to writhe and shake before becoming still. Chaz took his chance and ran for the woods.

6

Chaz was breathless.

He had run as fast as he could towards the wood or forest, he didn't care. Which was two or three hundred metres away from the poor wretched peasants, who, now free from the control of the hideous, one-eyed creatures who had enslaved them, were now shouting out in fearful voices to each other.

"Where the hell are we,'

As they backed away from a pile of rocks strewn round a large hole in the ground, they kept glancing at the blooded face of a hideous, one-eyed creatures' body, sprawled on the rocky pile.

Still panting hard, Chaz, arms clasped round a tree which was partially hidden by a large bush, *'Jeez, that was close.* '

Then, turning round, he began to make his way through the trees.

Progress was slow, since he had to force his way through dense ferns, nearly as tall as himself.

He noticed that he was going downhill, now at a faster rate, because of the staff he had trimmed from a slender branch with his jack-knife that thankfully, he still had in his jacket pocket.

(Now comfortably dry).

A glance up at the sky, through a gap in the tree tops, made him stop bashing a path through the dense ferns. It was getting dark, '*Damn,*' he thought.

'*I've got to find some shelter.*'

He looked around, through a gap in the trees, he saw a glade.

Forcing his way through the ferns which choked the space between the trees, Chaz found himself in a meadow-like clearing, with several broken branches scattered across it, lying in the grass and on the far side, a fallen tree, whose trunk was wedged against it's nearest neighbour, several metres above the forest floor.

'*Jeez, what luck,*' Chaz muttered to himself.

And he began to pick up the fallen branches. He had the makings of a simple lean-to shelter.

Once he had enough, trimmed with some difficulty, with his jack-knife. Chaz plaited some long grass to make a simple cord to tie together, a frame with the now trimmed branches.

Leaning it against the lower end of the fallen tree, Chaz cut and collected enough fern leaves to weave a wind and hopefully rain-proof shelter.

Although there had been a shower of rain earlier, his wet trainers were the proof of that, the grass under the fallen tree was dry enough for Chaz to lie down on.

Chaz sighed, as he sat inside of his rough shelter.

He was hungry and thirsty.

'Drink first,' he thought, as he looked out across the glade.

A troop of ants caught his eye, as they marched in line across the grass towards a very large tree, not to far from where he sat.

He shot upright, a sudden thought had come to him.

'Of course, the ants,' he called out.

Chaz got to his feet, and rushed towards the tree that the ants had just begun to climb in single file.

'What luck,' he cried.

And anxiously looked round his rough shelter.

The Gods were on his side.

Not far from where he was standing, he saw several Calabash gourds, sometimes called *'Bottle Gourds,'* he knew, lying in the long grass.

He bent down and picked one up and looked inside it.

'Gods be praised, empty and whole,' he thought.

And stuffing it inside his jacket. He began to climb big the tree.

A few metres up he found what he was looking for, a fork in the tree-trunk.

Just as he had hoped, it had a hollow centre. And it was full of rainwater.

The ants had reminded him of this natural phenomenon.

Carefully, Chaz lifted the bottle gourd from inside his jacket and wedged it between a convenient branch. Then, using his cupped hands, he first had several drinks of water.

'Bliss'

He was so thirsty he had several more, before he climbed slowly down to the ground, without spilling a drop from the filled gourd.

He proudly applauded himself, as he made his way back to the relatively safety of his shelter.

A short time later his stomach began to rumble, so Chaz slowly got to his feet and began to search the nearby bushes for something he could eat.

He was lucky enough to find a blueberry bush full of ripe fruit.

He made a *pig* of himself by eating so many, he was nearly sick.

Satisfied and eventually feeling much better, Chaz lay down on a pile of dried grass and began to doze.

It was nearly night-time he guessed, he had lost his watch ages ago and he fell asleep as the sun disappeared for the night.

7

All was still and quiet, when branches of the forest began to sway as a gentle breeze passed through them.

Then the upper branches began to weave to and fro as the wind grew stronger. Then, with sudden gusts, the trees above Chaz began to bend and shake with such force, that his make-shift shelter at ground level was also buffeted by a wind that shrieked and howled through the forest.

Chaz jumped to his feet and looked our of his shelter and saw a glow in the open space of the glade.

The wind was swirling round and round like it had no other place to go to, picking up fallen leaves and other forest floor detritus.

Chaz had to dodge a broken branch before it wacked him on the head,

The glow in glade was 33suddenly blocked by several flying animals descending to the ground.

Chaz shrank back and dived back inside his shelter, his homemade grass -cords tying it to the fallen tree, were fortunately strong enough to keep it intact against the now, terrifying gust of a whirlwind, racing round the glade.

'What the hell.'

The animals landed on the grass.

And the glow returned.

'I don't believe what I'm seeing,' whispered Chaz to himself.

Five large stags, each one carrying a beautiful girl with flowing, long-blond hair, and clad in bellowing cloaks.

They had control of the stags by holding snakes as reins.

'Jeez,' Chaz crouched even lower inside his shelter.

'They must be the Vella Nymphs, I'm in big trouble now.'

The nymphs dismounted and the stags walked to the far side of the glad and began to graze on the grass, the snakes slithered down from them and disappeared into the undergrowth.

Forming a circle, the nymphs began to sing. They had the most beautiful voices that Chaz had ever heard.

He suddenly felt a tremor go through his body, as the singing nymphs began to dance round and round.

Suddenly feeling weak Chaz, lay down in the shelter and his eye-lids began to close.

As the dancing nymphs began to twist and turn, faster and faster, their singing voices changed to a hypnotic, compelling rhythmic chant.

Chaz effected by this, stirred and shifted on his makeshift bed, before getting to his feet in a bewitched state. He was helpless, with no control over his actions.

An unspoken command ordered him to leave his shelter and join the swirling dancing nymphs.

Entering the circling gyrating, now singing nymphs, Chaz was forced into a series of whirling, leaping pirouettes with them.

The tempo never slackened and Chaz, unable to control his body movements was beginning to get physically tired.

Suddenly, four of the nymphs left the dance, leaving a very tired, weakening Chaz, with the last, single still singing, nymph.

8

The dance continued with just the two of them, as the other four nymphs, mounted their stags and at a command from one of them, pairs of snakes slithered up the flanks of the stag, along to the neck and took a hold on a snaffle with their mouths, thus becoming the reins.

Then, in unison, the four stags carrying the nymphs, leapt up into the air and disappeared through the glow that still covered the glade.

The fifth nymph started to chant as she danced round Chaz and he began to move faster and faster in a contrary circle to her

Chaz was feeling exhausted and he began to stumble and stagger as he blindly danced on.

The nymph, staring at him, began to smile to herself.

She knew what was about to happen to Chaz – *he was doomed to die,* as she chanted on.

The luxurious long blonde hair, was sinuously flowing behind the nymph, as she went to pass round in front of Chaz, when he lost his balance.

Unconsciously aware of what he was doing, Chaz tried to stop himself from falling by grabbing something

It was a single strand of the blonde hair of the nymph, that had flicked across his face as he fell.

The effect was immediate.

With a loud scream of agony, the nymph collapsed to the ground, writhing and twisting, her back then arched up and blood erupted from her mouth.

With one more twitch, here body lay still.

(The one and only way to kill a nymph was to full out a strand of their hair – Chaz had unintentionally done that).

The glow that had lit the glad began to dim, as the stag, with a snake draped around his neck, leapt up into the sky.

Chaz groaned and sat up, looking around the empty glade as the glow finally disappeared…

**

'Chaz, Chaz, wake up,' we've arrived at the Belogradchick railway station. Chaz's Uncle Brydon smiled happily.

A bemused Chaz sat up in the back seat of a decrepit taxi. A blackened and twisted tooth face of the taxi-driver smiled at him. '*Allo agin.*'

'What, what….?'

He looked down at the strand of blonde hair twisted in his hand.

Extra Bonus

Marco

Brian Leon Lee

A short story of how young Marco Polo, with the help of two reluctant time travellers, Chaz Lorimore and Esha Leung, was given the chance to become the famed, intrepid explorer of his time.

ISBN-13 9781079730449

Comtents

Chapter 1 5

Chapter 2 10

Chapter 3 14

Chapter 4 22

Chapter 5 25

Chapter 6 30

Chapter 7 35

Chapter 8 40

1

'Wow, what a f.... fantastic view,' Chaz Lorimore said, as he leaned closer to the apartment window and looked down forty-seven storeys, to watch the scurrying, ant-like people dash across a road junction before the lights changed.

He looked further down the road and saw serried ranks of similar high-rise apartment blocks as far as the eye could see.

Turning back into the room, he looked over to Esha Leung, a dark-haired veterinary assistant in the State Park Queensland, Australia and coughed into his hand.

'Err, it's a bit different from the Andes.'

'Esha gave a laugh and looked over at her Uncle Jinhai sitting opposite her at the dining table.

'Just look at him Uncle. He's actually blushing.'

'Now, now, Esha stop being a tease. From what you have told me, Chaz has never been to Hong Kong before.'

Jinhai Chen, a recently retired professor of chemistry, who was quite tall and still had a good head of silvery hair and a wispy moustache which now twitched, as he pointed to the dining chair opposite him and said.

'Take no notice of her Chaz. She is just behaving like that cheeky monkey I knew. What was it, Esha, ten - twelve years ago when you....'

'Don't you dare tell Chaz that story, he'll think I'm a moron or something worse.'

Chaz sniggered and got an elbow in his ribs as he sat down next to her.

'Now that you two have calmed down, try some of my herbal tea. Made from of seven different herbs, no less, plus my, what you say, magic ingredient.'

And he poured from an ancient looking porcelain teapot a golden stream of amber coloured liquid into their cut glass tumblers.

'While you are enjoying that, I'll go and get that bit of family history that we talked about, Esha. Okay.'

After a perfunctory sniff, Chaz took a sip and then another and then licked his lips.

"Bloody hell, it's got a kick like a mule. What did you say your uncle was, Esha?'

'A chemist, he was a Professor of Chemistry.'

Chaz and Esha had met up in Bolivia earlier that year. An unusual event had catapulted them, along with two other new friends, into a lethal, bitter conflict with, of all things, the Conquistadors of South America.

**(Spectre of El Dorado).*

Nobody believed them of course. So, after a week or two of coming back to reality, Esha suggested to Chaz, that maybe he would like to meet up with her in Hong Kong.

Her Uncle, she explained, had mentioned a few times that her family ancestry had connections with Dunhuang, a town on the Old Silk Road.

Chaz was intrigued enough to say that he still had a few weeks left of his end of Uni holiday and agreed to meet her in Kowloon.

Uncle Jinhai returned carrying an old, scruffy cardboard file and sat down opposite them, saying as he opened it.

'Most of what I have in here is not of much interest to you, Esha but when I came across a mention of a certain Jinhai Chen, my namesake would you believe, during the time of Marco Polo and that he was reported to have helped save his life, this is what I found.'

'Wow!'

Chaz pricked up his ears. At least he had heard of Marco Polo – who hadn't.'

'Have a look,' and her Uncle passed a tattered piece of discoloured parchment to her.

Esha took hold of the document, looked at it for a few seconds and then she suddenly cried out.

'I don't believe it. The writing, it's in old Mandarin script.'

As far as Chaz was concerned, it could have been in Double Dutch.

'So,' he said, 'What's special about that?' 'Well,' Esha leaned forward in excitement. 'To be able to write in Mandarin in the thirteenth century you had to come from the richer class or be a trained government official.'

She looked over to her uncle and pressed his arm.

'Oooh, do you think this Jinhai Chen could have been in charge of the Dunhuang caravanserai?'

'Maybe. What a nice idea but that is something that we shall never know, Esha.'

'Well, I want to go to Dunhuang, now more than ever. We might find out something more about this saving of Marco Polo. What do say Chaz?'

Chaz looked at Esha. He'd come this far, so what the hell.

'I'm in,' he said.

'Oh, I'm so glad,' she said, as she buried him in a pleasantly tight cuddle.

Uncle Jinhai smiled at them and then said, 'If that's the case, I have something that might be very useful. The Gobi Desert is full of all sorts of creepy crawlies.'

He stood and went over to a corner unit and

rummaged in it for a minute before picking up a slim narrow plastic box.

'It contains six sealed patches of antitoxin inhibitors that I developed before I retired. Unfortunately, lab politics got in the way of its commercial development. One of the reasons I retired,' he said ruefully, as he handed the box to Esha.

Being a veterinary assistant, Esha was well aware of the danger of catching nasty bugs and things and she stood and gave her uncle a hug of thanks.

*

Shortly after they had said bye to her uncle, Esha and Chaz were making their way down one of Hong Kong's giant escalators in order to catch a MTR (Mass Transit Railway) connection to their overnight hostel.

On the way down, Esha used her smart phone to book their rail tickets to Dunhuang via Lanzhou, a journey of around twenty-six hours.

As usual, Esha was chattering ten to the dozen and Chaz, not a great traveller at the best of times, gamely tried to keep his eyes open as well as avoiding bumping into what must be half of the world's population.

2

Chaz clung to the handrail of the carriage and eased himself down onto the station platform.

Du nhuang. They had actually made it. Jeez, what a journey. The least said about it the better, he thought. *Battery hens had more bloody space then this chuffin' train (No pun intended). The 'rail hard-sleeper' carriages – Who was the cretin that gave it that name – he was bleeding right about that though, had two lots of three narrow, wafer thin bunk-beds set in alcoves all along one side of the carriage. Each with a curtain for privacy, fortunately.*

Of course, brainbox had forgot that people bring luggage with them. So the passage was chock-a-block with stuff. It took a good twenty minutes of pushing, twisting and climbing to get to that crappy buffet-bar or toilet.

Jeez, the first soddin' time we went, they found out that you had to bring your own cup for any sort of drink, for God's sake. Sods law that he lost the toss of the coin and had to go back for the plastic cups they fortunately had in their daypacks left on their beds.

Fortunately, they had been given the two top ones. A great advantage Chaz found, was that his feet were able to stretch out over the corridor, way above anyone passing along it. a boon for the taller guy.

The occupants of the beds below had no extra room like that, as the alcove wall was in the way.

He thanked the Gods who had also arranged the four elderly Buddhists, on a holy visit to the Mogao Caves, near Dunhuang, to this alcove. They made great guards when he and Esha were both away. They had become her slaves when she gave each one a packet of rice cakes.

Four or was it five more time they had to do that soddin' trip. Nature waits for no one of course............

'Chaz, Chaz, are you okay, you look terrible.'

Esha grasped hold of Chaz by his arm tightly and he looked groggily at her.

'Uh. Oh, sorry. I think this trip is one step too far and he gave a great big yawn, followed by what he thought was a great big grin.'

'Don't look at me like that,' she snapped back.

'I'm just as tired as you. So just watch it okay.'

'Hey, hey, I didn't mean anything.'

They had both stopped in the middle of the crowded platform, blocking the way for several groups of travellers who had to part quickly in order to go around them. Many gave a disapproving glance at what they thought was unseemly behavior in public.

They stared at each other for a few moments and Chaz saw a twitch in one of Esha's eyes and he started to smile and she in turn broke into a grin and it was over.

The taxi only took five minutes to reach the grandly named Dunhuang Silk Road Hostel.

A further ten minutes later they were shown to their basic uni-like bedrooms, men to the left, women to the right.

Since they had arrived in Dunhuang just after eight am in the morning, they had agreed to catch-up on the lost sleep and then meet hopefully around 13 hours for a meal in the hostel buffet bar.

Of course, Chaz needed a knock or two before he called out that he'd be down soon.

They were both naturally refreshed after their sleep and ready for their first proper meal for over twenty odd hours.

He gave Esha a wave when he saw her by a window table and sat down.

'I recommend the yellow noodles with meat and vegetables but try this first, Chaz.'

Chaz picked up a chilled glass of a pale-yellow liquid and tasted it.

'Not bad, not bad at all. What is it? I seem to recall the taste but I'm not sure now.'

Esha smiled.

'Well, it's actually rather special and was first made in Dunhuang.'

She laughed as she said, 'Now don't throw up.

It's made by boiling apricot peel and of course some other secret ingredients.'

Chaz nodded and took another drink.

'As I said, not too bad., not bad at all.'

3

They left the hostel shortly after finishing their meal, feeling quite human again for the first time in ages.

It was hot, 30c plus and Esha was wearing a straw doŭli (conical) hat.

Chaz need no urging. As a redhead he knew the necessity of protecting himself in hot sunny conditions and his khaki jungle hat's wide brim did the trick.

Their sunglasses were also essential in cutting down the glare.

The weight of his daypack pulled at his shoulders and he eased one of the straps.

Esha had persuaded him to bring it, saying that in Bolivia she had learnt never to take anything for granted. You never know what you might need, was her motto from now on.

For once he didn't argue and had brought his along.

The clatter of an approaching engine made Chaz look down the road.

A shabby looking single decker bus had arrived, its windows, scratched and etched by years of sand-particles, blown by strong winds, which had blasted against them.

The destination plate, next to the driver, could just be deciphered through the mucky windscreen. It read in Mandarin – Crescent Moon Lake.

'Ooh aren't we lucky,' Esha said. 'That's one of the places I was telling you about, Chaz. Come on, there's a crowd already at the shuttle bus stop.'

They hurried the last fifty or so metres and Esha said, 'Even you Chaz, can't get lost on this bus trip. It only goes there and back.'

Chaz pretended to ignore that remark. He was more concerned by the pushy bastard behind him, who kept crowding his space. Then the cheeky bugger, would you believe, suddenly gobbed to the ground, just missing his foot.

'What the hell.'

'Shush Chaz, you'll cause a scene,' whispered Esha.

'Me. Me, cause a scene. He nearly spat on my boot.'

'You're in China. They do things different here.'

'So, I bloody well see.'

'Please Chaz keep it quiet.

The bus driver is looking at you. He won't let you on if you keep making a fuss.'

Jeez, it seems as though a terrorist would get more respect round here than me, thought Chaz but he held his tongue –just and they found their seats.

It was stifling inside the shuttle despite each side window's slider being open and damned uncomfortable, thought Chaz, as sweat dripped down his face.

No chuffin' air-conditioning either. Typical. What a place.

He fiddled with his daypack perched on his knee and prayed that the M15 goon driver up front would get going.

Esha unzipped a side pocket of her daypack and produced two hand-held battery-operated fans.

'Here Chaz, this should help,' she said, passing him one with a satisfied – I told you so – look on her face.

With as much grace as he could muster, Chaz took it and turned it on.

A gentle but cool breeze wafted his face and he laughed and gave her the thumbs up, feeling much better already.

Then the shuttle bus engine rattled into life and five minutes later they were trundling along a wide, arrow straight tree – lined boulevard towards the highest sand dunes Chaz had ever seen.

They were at least one hundred metres high.

The shuttle stopped some way short of them and Esha, having replaced the fans, said, 'It looks as if there is a barrier of sorts across the road.'

They let the rush of eager sightseers get off first and left the shuttle bus, just stopping to put their daypacks on.

Along the left side of the road, a line of vendor stalls and tents were trying to cater for the whims of the tourist, displaying a huge variety of bright and gaudy handicrafts.

Walking slowly, not only because of the heat, Chaz, casually eyed what was on offer. Of course the main theme was the Crescent Moon Lake. It was remarkable how much ingenuity had been used to incorporate the one idea. Then he paused.

'Hang on, hang on a moment, Esha.'

A scruffy, Bedouin type tent had caught his attention.

In fact, it wasn't the tent as such, more the figure squatting in the shade of the awning.

He wore a brightly patterned silk robe, with a red sash round his waist. A black, shallow flower-pot style hat covered the few lanks of silvery hair struggling to reach his shoulders. His hands, placed on his knees were hidden inside the wide sleeves of the robe.

A wispy goatee beard couldn't hide the million wrinkles that lined his face.

Something pulled him like a magnet towards the figure and the drone of a chant emanating quietly from the old man stopped as he looked up and saw Chaz.

It was the eyes. They were golden amber in colour,

so strange and hypnotic and the sudden glance from the old man, made Chaz shudder and stop.

'Hang on, hang on for a moment Esha,' he heard himself say.

Next to the squatting figure was a small brass table on top of which lay an ornate brass tray complete with a set of tiny tea bowls. Along with them was a small gaz stove gently heating a beautifully gilded kettle, from which came a plume of steam.

'I say Chaz, why have you stopped?' asked Esha, in a slightly annoyed voice as she walked back up to him.

'Fancy some tea.'

As it happened, Esha had a sudden thought that a bowl of Chinese tea was a great idea.

'I...' She stopped for a moment, unsure again, then a feeling of warmth and well-being rushed through her.

'What a good idea, Chaz, I guess we go inside. I can't see any chairs out here. I suppose there're inside the tent.'

-

The old man had pointed to the entrance of the tent and carefully picked up and carried the tray of tea things and followed them in. As he put the tray down on a larger brass table, he gave a toothed gap smile and said in Mandarin, 'I Sulu, welcome you to my humble abode. May your ancestors rest in peace.'

'Oooh, did you hear that Chaz. Oh, sorry, he has just made us welcome.'

'I bet,' he whispered. 'That's what he tells all of his customers. Just wait until he gives you the bill.'

'Quiet, he'll hear you.'

Esha was pleasantly surprised. The inside, carpeted though sparsely furnished, was as clean as one could expect, being right next to several huge sand dunes.

To the left as they entered were several cloth-covered stools, so they quietly chose a couple and sat down.

The old man fussed with the tea things after he had taken a small black cube of wood from a nearby chest.

'What the hell,' whispered Chaz as he saw the old man take a wicked looking knife from inside his robe and start to shave a few slivers of wood into the tea bowls.

'I'm not drinking that chuffin' brew, no way.' Chaz was gob smacked at what he was seeing.

'Oh my God,' Esha whispered back.'

'Don't you see, he's not Chinese. He's a Tibetan. That's not wood; it's a compressed tea block. It was so precious in Tibet that it actually became a currency.'

Chaz wasn't convinced but when the boiling water was infused with the – whatever – a sweet smell rose up from the black liquid – tea. It was tea and then he noticed a tiny dab of butter practically all melted floating on the top.

'Ugh.'

'Chaz,' whispered Esha.

'Close your eyes. It tastes better that way at first.'

He carefully took a sip.

Well, he was still on the face of the earth and he took another that emptied the bowl.

He actually attempted a smile of thanks to the old man who, would you believe, winked at him before clapping his hands.

Esha joined in. 'Well done Chaz. At least you didn't throw up like I did the first time I drank Tibetan tea.'

Feeling like he had just won a race, Chaz looked around the tent more carefully as Esha and the old man gabbed away in Mandarin.

He noticed a sort of alcove in the corner, covered with a curtain. He was sure that he had just seen a flicker of violet light behind it. So, getting up from his stool he slowly edged his way over and took a peek. The others never noticed. They were still talking ten to the dozen.

He nearly collapsed in shock. A brushed steel-frame with a translucent screen of about two metres by two meters square, was pulsating with a regular beat.

He went closer and saw along the bottom bar, some scuffed letters and numbers, ...

.eck- 24. . 9

'Naw,' he said to himself.

'It's impossible. A teleport portal here in 2019, I'm chuffin' dreaming. I know, it's that soddin' tea. I bet the old devil drugged us. Just wait till I tell Esha. She fell for it hook line and sinker.'

Just then he heard an explosion. It sounded as though it was coming from the Crescent Moon Lake area and he ducked out of the alcove.

'Chaz, Chaz.' Esha was standing facing the tent entrance shaking like a leaf, broken tea bowls and a steaming kettle by her feet.

'What's happening? What shall we do?'

4

Before he could speak the old man shouted out in Mandarin.

'You must leave. They may come here. Go.' And he pointed to the portal.

'It must be a terrorist attack,' Chaz called out to Esha. He had guessed what the old man had said and he rushed over to the stools and grabbed their daypacks.

'For God's sake move it Esha.'

The urgency in his voice broke the spell that had transfixed her to the floor, unable to move.

'W.... where to?'

'Never mind, just follow me,' and Chaz turned round and ran awkwardly, carrying their packs into the alcove with Esha two steps behind.

As they ran towards the pulsating screen, the old man screamed something out in Mandarin but Chaz fearing the worse, grabbed Esha by the hand and jumped through the pulsating portal, dragging a screaming Esha along with him.

The sandy ground was hard and Chaz was only able to keep on his feet because of Esha clinging like a limpet to his arm.

The smell of a decaying half-decomposed lizard swarming with ants and clouds of flies.

jerked Chaz back to his senses. They had landed in some sort of rubbish heap, which appeared to be part of an old pit of some kind.

A trench, lined with cut stone, headed up the slope of a sand dune from what appeared to be a stagnant pond. The scum had more or less dried out in the oppressive heat from the look of the hard crust of its surface.

'Ugh. Get us out of here, Chaz. It stinks like hell.' 'You don't have to tell me. I think the only way out is up so let's go.'

Then he had a thought.

'Just a minute, we need to know where we are.'

He turned round and was only just able to make out the pulsating portal in the brilliant sunlight, which was hidden behind a large gnarled saxaul tree. It was a wonder that it hadn't skewered them when they jumped through the portal.

'By the way Esha, what was the old man shouting when we left in such a hurry?'

'Well, it sounded like, be back before sunset.'

Chaz nodded as he handed her pack to her and thought the easiest way was to follow the trench up the slope of the sand dune.

'You know what Chaz,' Esha said, pausing for a breath. The dune was steeper than she thought.

'What.'

Don't be daft, how can a smell follow you?

Come on, I want to see what's on the other side of this dune.'

A few more minutes of panting up the slope it flattened out and they saw it.

'Look at that Chaz,'

Esha pointed ahead to a squat building lying a hundred or so metres away to their right.

The trench went straight towards it and as they hurried to the building the sound of running water came from it, followed by a monstrous stench.

'Oh my God,' cried Esha in disgust.

'That trench is the sewer of the caravanserai. I remember now. The camels are put in stalls along one side and their urine and stuff drops down into a sloping sewer and is carried away from the caravanserai site.'

'Jeez, do you mean to tell me that we have been walking by a stinking sewer for all this time. Hang on; I nearly dived into that chuffin' pond down there. Ugh, I feel sick.'

5

A line of camels was just entering the arched main gate, designed to be wide and high enough to accommodate a fully laden beast.

Esha was trying to remember what else she knew about a caravanserai and said,

'The main thing is the square, open to the sky courtyard. You need space to unload the goods and then to get the animals out of the hot sun, so the animal stalls go all round the inner wall. Remember Chaz, donkeys and horses are used as well to carry stuff. A well is usually in the centre of the courtyard, which makes sense when all the animals are all round the walls.

The merchants and their servants and guards, will probably have small rooms or niches above the animals. The Caravanserai owner will provide fodder for a fee of course...'

She was suddenly interrupted by Chaz, who shouted out.

'What the hell. Just look at that. Am I dreaming or what?'

He was pointing at a patch of green next to a crescent-moon shaped lake shimmering in the sunlight. Esha looked past the end of the Caravanserai and down towards a dip between the next huge sand dune.

Unbelievably, a lake had formed there. It was the shape that had caused Chaz to call out.

'It's got to be the same one as the one we know near Dunhuang but how....' he trailed off.

'The portal Chaz. It's got to be the portal. It actually worked.'

They looked down at the beautiful sight. No wonder so many paintings were made and photos taken. It was breathtaking.

'Yeah, we now know where we are but *when* are we?'

Esha was half petrified and exhilarated at the same time. 'Even if we know *when* we are, I don't want to spend the rest of my life here. Do you?'

Chaz kicked a small rock.

'Well, why don't we go and talk to someone in the Holiday Inn,' he said pointing to the Caravanserai.

'Don't get funny on me now Chaz, this is serious.' Esha bit her lower lip.

'Well at least you made a good suggestion, let's go and see what's happening.'

A rough looking guard holding the biggest sword Chaz had ever seen stopped them at the gate.

'Where are your camels?' he asked in old Mandarin.

Thinking fast, Esha turned and pointed to the lake.

'Down there with our family.'

The guard shrugged and moved aside and let them enter. He didn't even bother about their garb.

Travellers wore the most outlandish stuff these days, he thought. *Still, it's their choice.*

It seemed chaotic to them as they went under the arched entrance to the paved courtyard, past a stone staircase on each side, one leading to the office of the Caravanserai and the other to a series of anti-rooms for the Merchants and their servants.

Groups of merchants and servants were unloading pack animals. Horses were nuzzling nose-bags of food, camels kneeling as their loads were taken off.

A scurrying line of men carried sacks of goods to temporarily pile them against the courtyard walls between animal stalls and bays.

Shrill voices, echoing around the courtyard in several different languages, were arguing about prices or fees.

The smell of ordure permeated the air.

In the far corner of the courtyard, the travellers that Chaz and Esha had seen earlier, were sorting themselves out.

It seemed like organized chaos.

The head of the group could be heard shouting orders and directing his servants to do this or that.

'You won't believe this Esha but that guy over there is speaking in Italian.'

'Oh my God. It can't be, can it?'

'Give over, Esha, he's ancient. Fifty at least.'

'Yeah but are there any younger men there.' 'From what I can see from here, I think there are about nine or ten of them over there who might be fairly young looking for this time. Haven't you noticed? Look around you.'

Esha nodded and had a casual look round the courtyard.

Amongst the filth and dust that was being kicked up or being blown by the breeze that wafted in now and again, most of the men and she realized it was nearly all men, were bearded and wore a turban or hat of some kind. Their clothes, mostly ragged looking, apart from the merchants themselves, gave nothing away as to how old they might be.

'See what I mean.' Esha nodded again. 'It's hopeless, isn't it? I mean, we don't even know what year it is, apart from looking around here, which looks as though it's a period of the past. Right.'

Chaz could only agree.

To keep out of the way they moved to one side past the stone steps and stood by large bundles stacked by the wall.

As they did so, a tall man came down the steps carrying a scroll. A tuft of greying hair peeked out from the edge of his peak-less cap. A full beard was let down by a wispy moustache which gave him a whimsical expression.

The man stopped a couple of steps from the courtyard floor and called out, 'Signore Maffeo, Signore Maffeo.'

Among the group of travellers in the far corner of the courtyard, the leader turned round and waved.

'Yes, Jinhai Chen, what do you want?'

"I need an itinerary of your animals and men and of how long you intend to stay.'

'I shall be with you as soon as I have sorted these goods and animals.'

'Sooner rather than later please. We lock-down at sunset remember and I want to finish by then.'

Signore Maffeo acknowledged with a wave, as Jinhai Chen went back up the steps to his office.

6

'Jeez, did you hear that Esha.'

Chaz had grabbed her arm and rushed on in an excited voice.

'Maffeo, isn't that Marco Polo's uncle. My God, don't you see, we're actually in the time of Marco Polo. It's a chuffin' miracle, that's what it is, a chuffin' miracle.'

'Keep it down Chaz,' whispered Esha anxiously. 'That guard might hear you and get suspicious.'

She pulled at Chaz.

'Get down by these bundles for a minute, while I think.'

They crouched behind the pile of merchandise and looked to see if anyone was watching them.

Everyone was too occupied with their work to notice them and Esha relaxed somewhat.

'Chaz, Chaz,' whispered Esha. She had to nudge him for his attention.

He was preoccupied watching a horse relieve itself, fortunately over a slot in the courtyard floor, strategically placed there, for this very purpose.

'Oh, sorry, you don't see that every day where I llive. What is it?'

'You must have heard him. That Maffeo, he said Jinhai Chen. My uncle's name, remember.'

The penny dropped.

Chaz nearly jumped to his feet in excitement.

'That Jinhai Chen must be your ancestor, Esha.'

'Oooh, Chaz, does that mean that we will both disappear if I speak to him. You know, like in the movies.' Esha was half serious.

That wiped the grin off his face for a moment.

'Naw, I think that's just sci-fi stuff and nonsense. Anyway, that means Marco Polo must be around here doesn't it.'

They sat back against the wall in the shadow of a pile of stacked goods and watched for a while.

A sense of order could now be seen.

More and more of the animals were led into their allotted stalls, as they were unloaded. The piles of goods dotted around the courtyard were being transferred to niches and chambers set aside for them.

Chaz gave Esha a nudge. 'Do you see what I can see?'

'Stop playing games, Chaz,' she whispered

'At times you drive me mad with your innuendoes. Just tell me.'

He gave a shrug and half pointed across the courtyard.

'See that bloke, wearing a grey tunic over a white shirt and those sort of, tight-leggings. He's got one of those floppy hats on, you know, with a bit hanging over one ear.'

Esha looked over through a group of snuffling, grunting camels and saw him walking towards the gateway and nodded.

'Well, from what I saw of his face he can't be very old.'

A flicker of excitement went right through her body, as she leaned closer to Chaz.

'What do you mean?' 'He's got practically no beard to speak of or moustache. It's no more than a wispy goatee. I reckon he's about twenty years old.'

'Chaz, that must be Marco, must be,' she said, crossing her fingers. Nodding his head in agreement, Chaz pointed to the gateway and said quietly.

'We need to follow him but not too close. We stand out like sore thumbs with our modern clothes on.'

Esha looked around. Not far from the stone steps three, maybe four bundles of cloth were stacked, seemingly waiting for someone to take them away.

Checking that no one was looking their way, Esha eased her way over and saw what she had hoped for – a hole in the bundle.

A piece of white silk could be seen, so finger on lips to Chaz, Esha opened her daypack and found a small pair of scissors in a side pocket.

Then she beckoned to him. 'Help me pull this out,' she said, indicating the silk. The sacking was tough but with a few snips with the scissors, Esha made the hole big enough for Chaz to pull a bolt of white silk out.

'What are you going to do with this?' asked a perplexed Chaz.

'Watch and learn,' smiled Esha as she unrolled a length of the white silk, measuring with her eyes.

Using her scissors, she cut a long piece off and held it to his body and nodded to herself.

'Just hold it out for me please Chaz,' she asked.

As he did so, Esha cut two slits in the sheet of silk. 'Now for the moment of truth,' she muttered.

'Put this on like a bath robe, Chaz,' she instructed, going back to her daypack while he did so.

With his hands through the slits, he now had a robe of sorts reaching nearly down to his boots, especially when fixed by the neck with the safety pin she had just got from her pack. Most of his modern clothes were now largely hidden.

It took her only a minute or two to make one for herself.

'I believe they used to call this sort of thing a Surcote,' she said, as she fastened it by her neck with another safety pin.

7

By the time they had passed the guard at the Caravanserai entrance, Marco, for they were now convinced that was who he was, had disappeared.

'Sod it,' Chaz said, with a groan of disappointment.

'Where the hell can he have got to?'

Esha looked left and right along the rough track made in the loose sand.

'There's only one place he could go,' she said with conviction.

'The moon lake.'

So, turning to the left, they made their way along the outside wall of the Caravanserai until they reached the end of it. The dune suddenly dipped and there, a couple of hundred metres in front was Marco striding down the slope towards the oasis.

The dune levelled out in a sort of platform, which was covered with a dense mix of saxaul and tamarix bushes, many three or four metres high. The unusual shaped lake was some twenty-five metres further down a gradual slope of the dune.

Esha and Chaz crouched down, hoping not to be seen, as they watched Marco force his way through the thicket of bushes towards the lake.

They were not sure what they were going to do when - if, they actually caught up with him.

Something happened by the lake.

A loud shout echoed round the dunes and Chaz stood up to get a better view.

'Can you see what's happening, Chaz?' Esha said, getting to her feet.

'It looks damn funny to me,' he replied. 'Marco's waving his arms about. Just a minute, now he's dancing.'

'What! He's dancing?' asked Esha incredulously.

'Sorry, that's wrong, not dancing. Jumping. Jumping like the devil.'

As they watched the cavorting figure of Marco by the edge of the lake, he suddenly screamed out, a cry of pure agony.

'My God, what the hell's happening? We have to go down and help him, Chaz,' cried Esha, who had already begun to run down towards the lake.

Chaz needed no more urging. The high-pitched cry in Italian, which went on and on without pause, drove him like a bat out of hell.

He overtook Esha and forced a way through the tangle of bushes until he reached the edge of the lake.

Marco lay writhing in obvious agony on the sand, his face covered with sand flies and both hands clutching his ankle in a vice like grip.

Next to him was a small snake, it's head crushed by the bloody rock, which lay by his feet.

Esha arrived, panting heavily.

'How is he?' She asked between breaths.

Then she saw the snake. *A pit viper,* she thought.

Staying calm, her work as a veterinary assistant could prove the difference between life and death.

'Quick as you can Chaz, try and get his hands off his ankle and lean him against the trunk of that big bush while I get that box of antitoxin inhibitors that Uncle Jinhai gave me from my pack. My God, he must have second sight or something.'

As fast as she could, Esha threw off her makeshift robe and pulled the pack off her shoulders.

Chaz had bent down and tried to waft away the swarm of sand flies that had settled on Marco's face, unable to avoid watching Marco twitching in agony as the venom began to take hold.

He scratched at his own face as he began to get bitten and then managed to loosen Marco's grip on his ankle. As gently as he could, he then put his hands under his arms and lifted him side-ways to the bush that Esha had indicated.

Marco groaned and began to breathe rapidly.

'Scuse me,' Esha said, as she pushed past him. 'We haven't much time. Pull up his leggings, carefully now. We mustn't move him too much.' As soon as the ankle was free, Esha picked out one of her uncle's purple patches of antitoxin inhibitors. Removing the purple covering she placed the patch gently over the nasty snake-bite puncture wound. Esha looked over at Chaz.

'Uncle Jinhai told me this was very special and effective if put on as soon as possible after the bite. The patch will, he told me, dissolve by itself. That it was part of the treatment. It mustn't be touched before then, so I'd better cover it with something to hide what I've done.'

Esha delved into her pack again and pulled out a linen shirt and with a shrug, cut a strip from it.

Having tied the bandage, *she couldn't leave a twenty-first century safety pin;* She looked at Chaz and said, 'Now I will have to report this to the Caravanserai. They will have to look after Marco from now on.'

Chaz started to protest.

'Only I can speak old Mandarin. I have to go. You look after Marco, okay.'

That had to make sense to him, so he nodded in agreement as Esha put her pack and then her white silk Surcote on and ran up the sand dune towards the Caravanserai as fast as she could.

8

At first, the Caravanserai manager, Jinhai Chen ignored her plea to bring Marco up from the lake.

He had just come down the stone steps by the gateway and was getting annoyed by Esha's persistent requests for help. *Women should not be here,* he thought, *they get in the way of the efficient running of a Caravanserai.*

She had a funny way of speaking as well, a dialect he found difficult to understand. Then he recognized the word

Jinhai Chen paused. Signore Maffeo was an important traveller. He carried the seal of the Great Kublai Khan. Thinking he had better check this out, Chen sent a message requesting the presence of Signore Maffeo.

He came at once.

When Esha explained the urgency of Marco's injury to Signore Maffeo, all hell broke loose.

Two guards were summoned and ordered to select a camel chair at once and to carry it down to the lake.

Signore Maffeo in his anxiety, grabbed Caravanserai Chen by the arm and gave orders for him to be taken to Marco at once.

A flustered Chen looked at Esha and said, 'You will have to show us where to go.'

A much relieved, Esha, just nodded and rushed to the gateway, the others following as best they could.

***

Chaz was getting anxious. Esha seemed to have been gone for ages. He had wet his handkerchief in the lake and dabbed Marco's forehead with water.

Worryingly, Marco did not stir. He just lay there propped up by the gnarled trunk of the bush, sweat beading his face.

A rustling sound and voices broke the silence. Chaz stood just as Esha and the elderly man known as Maffeo burst into view, followed by Chen and the two guards who had trouble pulling the camel chair through the branches of the bushes.

'Marco, Marco.' Uncle Maffeo fell to his knees and grabbed hold of Marco's hand.

'Marco,' he called again.

Esha suddenly called Chen to her and whispered something to him. Chen shook his head but Esha insisted and pointed to the dead snake.

This time he nodded and said, 'Signore Maffeo we must take Marco to the Caravanserai at once if you want to save his life.'

Marco's uncle saw the sense in that and ordered the two guards to put Marco in the camel chair that they had carried down. The cane chair, one of a pair that are usually fixed on the camel back-to-back, was big enough for Marco to be strapped in and it also incorporated a foot-rest, so that his legs would be securely tied as well.

Esha standing next to Chaz, was relieved to see that. She was aware that snake-bite victims were not to be moved unless absolutely necessary.

The two guards went to pick up Marco who had still not uttered a sound, when one stopped and handed a short sword to Chen and indicated that he go first and chop a way through the thicket of bushes.

Chen nodded and immediately began to hack a way through, wide enough for the guards carrying Marco to safely follow when they were ready.

Uncle Maffeo went next, muttering to himself in Italian, some sort of prayer.

Progress was slow up the dune but eventually they reached the Caravanserai without any accidents and as Esha and Chas watched, Marco was taken inside.

Before Chaz could say anything, Esha turned and pointed to the sun. It was sinking behind the huge dune on the far side of the Crescent Moon Lake.

'It can't be that late,' cried Chaz in amazement. 'We haven't been here that long surely?'

'I'm not going to argue but remember what the old man Sulu, said,' answered Esha.

'Yeah and now we're up shit creek without a chuffin' paddle. What the hell do we do now?'

'Come on Chaz; think for God's sake. How did we get here?'

'Of course. The portal. We've got to get to the portal.'

Esha smiled to herself. 'I knew you'd get there eventually Chaz.'

'Now who's being funny. Come on we don't have much time. That's assuming the damn thing is still there and it still chuffin' works.'

'Don't say that, Chaz.' For the first time Esha felt uneasy and anxious.

Going down the sand dune made it easier and quicker than the first time they had come this way.

The stone lined sewer trench was easy to follow. The stench coming from it didn't smell any better the second time round.

As they walked down, Esha remembered the

document written by this historical Jinhai Chen.

'I say Chaz, that old document that my uncle showed us.'

Yeah, what of it?'

'Well, in the excitement of knowing who he might be, I sort of glossed over some of the things he had written.'

'Such as,' prompted Chaz.

'We know from history, that Marco stayed in Dunhuang for about a year after getting over an illness. Well, this Jinhai Chen wrote that two passing Shamans helped heal a lethal foot injury of Marco Polo and that one had red hair and who never spoke and the other was a woman with a hunch-back.'

'So,'

'Look at us Chaz what do you see.'

'Err, two dirty faces,'

'Chaz, for God's sake be serious for once.'

'Okay, okay,' he grinned and said, 'we both look like a pair of monks lost in the wilderness with these white silk robes on.'

Then the penny dropped.

'Jeez, you've a bump on your back. The daypack. Of course, he never saw you without these robes on did he?' Chaz said, patting her on the back.

'Chuffin' hell, what a carry on.'

'Yes, because of your size, yours didn't stick out as much as mine. '

'So, you're the mystery female Shaman.'

'I suppose I am,' Esha said, bowing to her red-headed assistant before reflecting; 'That's if we ever get back.'

That shut Chaz up for a while until they reached the stinking pond.

'It must be round here somewhere,' Esha said apprehensively, looking at every bush in sight.

The sun had reached the top of the dune on the other side of the hollow they were in, making long shadows of the saxaul bushes.

Chaz felt the tightening of his stomach and taking a deep breath, turned round, fingers crossed in the age- old belief of hope in adversity.

There, in the shadows a flicker of light – a violet light.

'Hallelujah, cried Chaz.

'There is a God after all. Look Esha, over there. It's the portal. Come on let's get the hell out of here. Now.'

The gnarled saxaul branches hid most of the portal but the flickering light was as good as a flaming beacon as far as Chaz was concerned as they went behind the bush.

Holding Esha by the arm, he jumped first over the edge of the portal pulling her through as he did so.

And landed on the carpet inside the tent.

The old man was just picking up the last of the broken tea bowls and he straightened up, smiling.

He bowed towards them, unfazed by the fact that they were still wearing the makeshift white silk robes.

'I Sulu, welcome you back to my humble abode. I trust you had an eventful journey. I see from the look on your faces you did. It was well that that you took my advice and left before sunset. You were very wise to do so.'

The old man called Sulu put the broken pieces of porcelain on the table and said, 'I too have a journey to make and must say goodbye to you.'

He held up a hand - palm outwards - fingers together with the thumb tight to the fingers.

Then he opened the middle two fingers into the peace sign and said in a voice that could hardly be heard.

'May your ancestors rest in peace?

Then he walked to the portal and jumped through to another place and another time.

It was as though someone had turned a switch. The tent began to shake and shudder and Chaz suddenly had a funny feeling.

'For God's sake move,' he shouted to Esha.

As if coming out of a dream, Esha suddenly

screamed as she saw the top of the tent suddenly collapse and begin to fall down towards them.

There was nothing to do but run and she ran to the entrance.

Chaz needed no more urging either and he ran after her and they both stood by the roadside and gaped in disbelief as the whole shabby mass of the tent fell into a whirlpool of dust and sand, which then became a flickering, discharge of electrical energy, that for a moment, dazzled them in its intensity, before fading away.

A clear patch of sand was all that remained when they regained their vision.

'What the hell was all that about,' Chaz said, scratching his head.

I've not the faintest idea Chaz but I know what I fancy now. A few glasses of apricot-peel water mixed with vodka or maybe that new Japanese whisky.

'Now that is what I call a good idea,' agreed Chaz as they began to walk on past a newspaper display board.

One caption caught his eye. It was a picture of the Crescent Moon Lake with a cloud of dark smoke drifting over it.

'I say Esha, what's that about?'

'Just a minute while I see,' she said.

'Oh, it says that a gaz cylinder explosion

caused little damage. A small fire was quickly extinguished.'

'So that was what scared us to death. Hey, without that we might never have met up with Marco. What a chuffin' coincidence.'

'Come on Chaz, I'm dying for that drink.'

'My God, I don't believe it,' he suddenly cried out as he jumped to get out of the way of someone who was in a hurry.

'That cretin has just gobbed on my boot.'

***